CLASH

by **Fouzia SOUALEM**

Translated from French by Fouzia Soualem

Copyright © 2022

978-2-958-161262

Legal deposit, December 2022

I dedicate this news to all the many people, they will recognize themselves, who believed that their vile actions could ultimately destroy me. To all those who took advantage of my generosity, my empathy, who believed that by treating me with condescension, they would be enhanced. To all these people, I advise henceforth, in addition to a good psychoanalysis, to go their own way and to expect nothing more from me.
But I would be magnanimous, and I thank them for their warranty because in the end, all their hatred and malevolence ended up bringing all the Light that was in me before I knew them.
I am back to being Me and I wish anyone who has gone through such a path to get up stronger and happier than ever.

TABLE OF CONTENTS

I WIND OF MADNESS

Everything changed because of a crumpled piece of paper which fell out of a trouser pocket, just before being washed in the washing machine.

And yet, the day had started well, it was hot, birds were singing, cats were jumping to do their job.

Like everyday life.

Until that wasteless moment that would radically change my life forever.

I was quietly picking up the laundry when I saw this insignificant paper falling to the ground. I could have done it mechanically a thousand times, but this time, I don't know why, I was intrigued.

Furthermore, I opened it and recognized clearly my husband's writing, Thomas' writing.

An appointment at a hotel had been doodled.

I dropped the laundry to the ground and opened my computer : it was located at the end of the town.

I couldn't believe my eyes.

After 15 years of marriage, I realized that my husband was cheating on me calmly.

In broad daylight, it might be one of his employees, he was a car dealership owner.

I was now looking out the window : he was joking with the neighbor.

He was proposing his help to trim the hedges next Sunday.

No, no, my dear, I think you'll have something else to do this Sunday.

I chose to wait patiently, very patiently, until he finished waxing the neighbor's pumps, and then I called him.

He went up the stairs rapidly, he looked happy as a lark.

I threw his draft in his face.

He picked it up when he read it, I saw a short hint of remorse in his eyes.

But the man pulled himself together quickly, and a lyrical flight followed.

The offended husband's plea :

" How can you doubt me? After all I've done for you …" (Well, I really didn't know what he could have done for me, and this, throughout our marriage).

"You should trust me, I swear I will never cheat on you with another woman!".

In short, trivialities.

But in context, it caught my attention.

This precision was strange, even for him.

He never took his eyes off me, waiting for me to let my guard down.

Too bad for him, I had slept rather well, and I was in full possession of my faculties right now. After a long hour of delirium, he sat down, looking serious, and told me : "I have to tell you something… It's not easy for me, but you deserve the truth. In fact, I didn't mean to hurt you".

The discussion was getting interesting.

I was about to know the lucky one. Afterwards, he could pack up and get out of my field of vision.

"After our baby's death, when I found her laying down on the chest in her cradle, I was in shock.

And yet, you knew you had to let her lay on her back and so, I blamed you for that. You destroyed our family so foolishly.

The poor baby must have suffered so much, unable to call for help.

Currently, I even thought to commit suicide."

I was stunned.

Once again, he was playing the guilt card, as he used to do for 12 years.

I never let my baby lie on the chest, but he found her so, and this tragedy took away my desire to be a mother one more time.

I didn't say anything.

He continued.

"I consulted a psychiatrist, you know him, Manuel, and one thing leading to another, we fell in love.

He helped me to feel better, you were crying all day long. You must understand. It was the only way, I wanted to avoid leaving you alone.

I realized I was fed up with women, sorry, I'd rather tell the truth right now".

It was getting better and better!

So, he's been cheating on me for 12 years, with a man, his psychiatrist, and it seems as if I have to thank him now!

I took a deep breath.

What should I answer about these cascading revelations?

"I think you should leave the home quickly".

But he disagreed, he was going to break up with his boyfriend. I didn't see the point of it, in fact.

I had endured his mood swings because I always felt guilty, he made me feel guilty, but now, it was the drop of water that made the vase overflow.

He awakened buried feelings for so many years.

In fact, it's a clever idea to make the other feel guilty about everything.

So, you can do what you want, it's surely because of the other person.

Well, everyone can't be rotten, vicious, heartless, but more people than we think can.

Isn't humanity's story proof of that?

And I hit the jackpot, I was living with one of these vicious specimens without even knowing it …

Was I so stupid? More naive than the majority of women?

Had I really laid my baby down on the chest?

And even if I was so exhausted that I did it, wasn't it my husband's role to support me instead of betraying me?

No way, I won't live with this usurper, this manipulator anymore.

Thoughts were jostling in my head, and Thomas was already calling Manuel, he put the loudspeaker.

Manuel disagreed, he shouted and cried, but Thomas was also so.

He left the house for a few days, he wanted to give me time to think over.

A sweet attention.

I didn't know what was to happen, I didn't know what I had to do, and even if I should do something.

My head was on the verge of exploding. My life had definitely no meaning.

Or maybe I was unable to give meaning to my life. Who knows?

I collapsed on the sofa, in the dark, curtains drawn.

When will this awful day end?

I couldn't sleep. I switched on the TV to feel less alone.

Later, while I was sleeping, it seemed to me that someone knocked at the door.

I turned around and hid my head under the pillow.

I was surely dreaming.

But then I heard the doorbell.

Its sound was so strong, it must have been created to warn of the arrival of the devil or something like that.

If it was the devil, he was late, he narrowly missed his twin brother.

So, I opened the door.

Its real face was a surprise : Manuel.

I let him enter, I was neither vindictive nor even angry.

I was just exhausted.

On the other hand, he was enraged, he couldn't be left that way, and he wanted to get it off his chest.

And I was willing to listen to everything.

He didn't say anything about his love story with my husband.

He just wanted to talk about my baby.

Not only that, but he clearly wanted to get revenge, but I wondered how.

During Thomas' psychiatric sessions, my dear husband confessed to him that HE laid down the baby on the chest himself. He was fed up with her screams at night, with his wife waking up each time to rock her.

And dawn, he went to the room, what was unusual in fact, and he shouted when he found her dead.

I was there, fixing him, hoping to have misunderstood and at the same time, relieved not to be guilty.

It was unprecedented violence, I felt horrible chest pain and my leg hurt as never.

He wanted me to lay down, he wanted to call for help.

Oh no, I just wanted him to repeat his story. He did it.

At the end, I pleaded with him to come out, calmly, very calmly.

During these 12 years, I was persuaded to be responsible for my child's death, I suffered martyrdom, when in fact my dear husband was the murderer. And he accused me to make feel guilty every day of my life.

He was looking me in the face for 12 years, lying to me.

I've been living with a criminal who found an excuse to cheat on me with his own psychiatric.

I didn't know what to do, I didn't know when I would do something, but when I collapsed in my rocking chair this night, I didn't cry, I didn't throw anything in the room.

Furthermore, I was incredibly calm, and I knew that after this night, I would know what to do.

II FORGIVENESS WILL SET YOU FREE

I woke up clearly, took a shower, aired the house, I even picked up roses in the garden to adorn a vase.

Beautiful yellow roses, their bright color could have cheered up any depression.

Then I began to diffuse this soft gardenia's perfume all over the house.

You feel better in a scented house.

And I sat down on my favorite chair, took a breath just before calling Thomas : he had to come fast.

The bigger compiled without asking questions.

He looked so shy when he entered the living room, as a child waiting for punishment after having done something stupid.

I offered him a coffee, he took it without a word.

It had to end.

"Listen to me Thomas, I couldn't sleep this night, I thought about all this story.

I really understand that what I've done traumatized you and that's why you found some comfort with Manuel, I can't reproach it to you.

He interrupted me :

— I'm so sorry, if only…, his eyes were full of tears.

— No, no, I really understand, I insisted, putting down my cup violently on the table.

I must take it upon myself now. You can't leave Manuel now, after all that he's done for you throughout these years.

— I don't understand, he stammered

— I think you should reconnect with him, apologize, and he will forgive you.

Firstly, we'll stay married, it will give you time to end your therapy, and without this secret, you will soon feel better, won't you?

He lowered his head.

I continued : It's awful to carry secrets, it's a good thing that the truth has come out.

I just beg you to be discreet, for the surroundings, you surely understand what I mean.

— Of course. I'll never thank you enough to be so comprehensive.

And he headed toward me, like a child toward Santa Claus.

I raised my arm to stop him.

— Don't exaggerate, Thomas, it's hard for me. I'll let you talk to Manuel."

With that, I took my car in the direction of the nearest massage parlor.

He didn't waste his time, he ran to join his lover and begged him to forgive him.

I almost choked or laughed when I thought about this dear Manuel who betrayed his lover's secret the day before!

There is a proverb which advises turning his tongue 7 times in his mouth before talking.

I know someone who may be thinking about it strongly now.

I laid down for my massage, my phone just in front of me, in vibrating mode.

Furthermore, I was staring at it, waiting.

10-9 : A desperate man will soon call me.

1-0 : this was the start of vibrations, which were about to last one hour.

Likewise, I enjoyed this sound while my masseuse was annoyed, without daring to say anything.

It was my best day in a spa in my whole life.

I choose to wait for my lunch break to listen to my messages. At the beginning of the afternoon, I called Manuel, he needed to see me urgently.

I took a look at my diary.

Yes, I had a free shot at four. We'll meet in a distant brewery.

Obviously, he was on time. And I was late, naturally.

I sat down and ordered a banana split (it was hot!).

Manuel was looking dismayed.

"Thomas apologized and said you accepted our love connection and…

I interrupted him :

— So, what's wrong?

He whispered.

— I confessed to you that your husband killed your baby and blamed you during all your marriage, and you would like to make me believe that you forgive him!

— I think you're worried, you fear he discovers you're not as reliable as he thinks you are, I said coldly.

No problem, I'll be magnanimous, it's clear that he's happy with you. For me, my marriage died with my baby. Our union was a kind of masquerade, and thanks to you, it's finished.

I just asked Thomas to stay discreet.

We'll separate officially in a few months, I have to think over my future. I'm thinking of moving on…

— I'll do all that you want, but please, never tell him what I told you! I was the only one to know the truth

— If you can share your life with a child's killer, I think you don't fear anything.

— Promise-me…

— I won't promise you anything, a psychiatrist sleeping with his patient over 10 years isn't worth trusting.

I wonder what would the council of order say about that ?"

He bowed his head, shaking his legs nervously under the table, I posed my hand on his shoulder and I got up.

"Keep calm, as long as you stay at your place, everything will be alright. After the divorce, I will not care for your pranks, your sneaky and unhealthy secrets, you both will go out of my life".

I left, relieved.

I came back home and I noticed Thomas Phone. His secretary had left a message, talking about something urgent, a car's delivery.

Suddenly, I realized I hadn't seen my in-laws for a long time : It was time.

The next day was devoted to shopping and cleaning up the house and at 18, my in-laws were standing at the door.

They made themselves comfortable, waiting for Thomas.

The apéritif was dragging on.

His mother was very conventional, and so, she was very upset :

"For once, we came, he could have been on time! We drove so long !" I had to temper things, he surely had an excuse. I called him, but he didn't pick up the phone.

His father was at his wit's end and took my phone, he called his son again and again and finally, Thomas answered, furious, he was shouting.

"Ok, leave me alone, I am working.".

My stepfather was flabbergasted. He dropped my cell phone, I was resigned and picked it up, before saying :

— Thomas, you shouted at your father, you know your parents are waiting for you for dinner.

A great silence followed, then I put the loudspeaker, and he continued :

— But what the hell are they doing here?

— We invited them, have you forgotten ?" And I hung up the phone.

His parents were annihilated, his father took me in his arms.

I was thinking to myself : "If only you knew what your offspring can do".

We began to eat dinner without him. He came back only at 22. I didn't know where he really came from.
He couldn't stop to apologize, he feared at the idea of his parents knowing the truth.

He explained he had a massive job's problem. Furthermore, he missed a significant message for a car's delivery and his client was furious and wanted to retract.

He realized nobody was ready to believe his story.

After his parents went to bed, he apologized once again while I was washing the dishes and asked me :

"When Did we decide to invite them, I really don't remember at all?

— You had this idea weeks ago, and we chose this date together.

It was difficult for me, but I kept the date, you could have tried.

And, by the way, I also have a job, I'm only on holiday".

His parents stayed a few days, they never stopped thanking me for all I was doing to save my marriage, their son was quiet, he always seemed elsewhere.

Each night, he escaped to be with Manuel.

They saw clearly in his game, and a discomfort invaded the house.

I continued to play my role of perfect housewife, discreet and smiling.

My in-laws were admiring, they had a lot of affection for me.

The day follows each other and look alike during this beautiful summer.

Thomas was more and more upset, he forgot everything, where he left his parcel receipt.

 He threw away the memos on the fridge and then was looking for them. He didn't care for his customers orders, blamed his secretary and yet so far, he always said she was the best one.

I told Manuel about that, and he prescribed him an antidepressant to help him go through difficult times.

My dear husband suffered so much!

Our doctor, for his part, knew that insomnia was making him aggressive and endangered his company.

He had to take sleeping tablets, but he refused.

I had to show ingenuity, this poor man had to sleep, the lack of sleeping is dangerous for health.

And, as a devoted wife, I had to do something to help him to go back up the slope.

III DEAR TRUST

I explained To Manuel the situation and the doctor's position.

He worried about mixing sleeping tablets and antidepressants, but I managed to convince him.

It's true that he feared losing his noble work, it waited a little in the balance, I think.

He proposed to slip sleeping tablets into his glass every night.

I found this idea pretty good, it all depends on the drink in fact.

So, Tomas' future was sealed, in a renowned psychiatrist's hands. He will care with a master's hand

for the medical prescriptions, so I'll have more time for my roses and my piano lessons.

Vengeance wasn't really in my ways of customs.

Thomas continued to go working, he sometimes launched at home to save appearances.

At night, he always stayed at Manuel.

I was thinking over what they were doing together, curled up in my bed, watching some of my poor

little baby's photographs.

At maternity, in her little cradle at home, in my arms in her pink diaper with white polka dots…

I spent my evenings crying, sleeping on the photographs. Occasionally, I hesitated for a long time,

holding the sleeping pills in my hand. I wanted to end, my whole life was an awful masquerade, I

married a torturer in costume who never loved me.

I rehashed Manuel's confession again and again. Occasionally, I was so exhausted that I felt all this

was untrue, just impossible.

At other times, I wanted to strangle them both : my husband killed my baby, he ripped out my heart,

treating me as an unworthy mother for all.

And his sidekick took advantage of the situation and kept the secret until he was betrayed in turn.

Which kind of person could do that?

Is every human capable of such perversion, such indifference?

Will all dads become crazy?

When I crossed a man going for a walk with his baby, first, I found it touching.

And I recovered, thinking he was insincere, walking as long as possible to draw attention, then he surely will swing him home in a place where he will not disturb him.

I desperately needed help. But no therapist could have helped me, I couldn't confess his crime, and if I did, how could he help me? How could he transform all this suffering? Thanks to barbiturates making me feel like a zombie?

No, clearly, there was no answer to my problem.

And when everybody will know the truth, everyone will laugh at me. It was.

How could I face my pupils again, the rumor will always precede me?

The sheepish Thomas had already disappeared.

He was convinced to have married the perfect idiot and so, I had no remorse to drive him crazy.

I didn't care if he lost his company, money didn't make us happy, money made him greedy and self-centered. Unless his ignominy was engraved in his DNA.

One evening, one of his clients came home. I was surprised, it never happened, in fact.

He was making excuses for disturbing me, but he was looking for Thomas in vain.

Normally, I would have driven him away, telling him to wait until tomorrow morning to call the secretary.

But, this evening, I felt I had to listen to him.

Instead of having dinner alone, I invited him and explained he had ordered and paid for a car, which should have been delivered 15 days ago.

But this was not the case and Thomas was never vacant at work, his secretary had no plausible explanation : he was sure to get scammed.

I pretended to be shocked, no, my husband was reliable, his reputation was solid, he would never steal anyone.

Well, I must confess that I had drunk several glasses before telling this.

It's true that some orders had mysteriously disappeared from his bag, first, Thomas blamed his secretary and even Manuel where he spent more and more time.

The truth is that mixing sleeping tablets and depressants had consequences.

At least, I thought so.

But how could I be sure of what Manuel was really doing?

My husband was losing his luster, he was more and more short-tempered, the poor forgot his appointments, made accounting mistakes, even his lover was losing patience with him.

By chance, I crossed his secretary. She was getting out of the supermarket as she did each Wednesday at 13.

She looked so upset that I invited her for lunch at the store gallery.

Furthermore, she confirmed that the car dealership was at its worst. I pretended to be surprised because my dear husband didn't tell me anything about this.

She added that Thomas' "oversights" and truculence had led to a point of no return.

She had been fired and was not the only one.

Not only that, but she asserted something : before, he gave her the instruction to forward calls to Manuel's landline in the evening.

She lowered her head, saying that he switched off his cellphone to avoid me.

At bottom, clients called in the evening, and the deliveries' appointments took place after 17.

Home's delivery was the company's spearhead.

Customers came, shouting at her in the morning because the order wasn't honored, her boss was always busy : she couldn't do anything.

I deduced that neither Thomas was losing his mind, nor Manuel was taking liberties with his phone.

One day, I went to his medical office, he had no choice but to receive me.

I told him about this calls' story, and he answered that he was getting tired of Thomas, who was hard to live with.

Here then…

But it was strange that he refused to answer to his customers, he let his company sink.

He confessed to have "maybe" deleted one or two messages mistakenly, but not more.

I was staring at him, feelingless, I think.

It was becoming hard to know who was playing with whom.

Was finally Manuel as unbalanced as Thomas?

He said that Thomas was waiting for the divorce to reconvert, and he was sinking the company to let me do nothing.

He added that his dose of sleeping tablets was small and couldn't affect his faculties.

Furthermore, he even thought that without the antidepressant, Thomas would be out of control.

He was talking about leaving him, but I reminded him he had to assume his choices, at least until the divorce.

He agreed, but admitted he considered committing him to a mental asylum.

Tell me who was the crazier of the two? Soon, it will not be my problem anymore.

      I left, more lost than when I arrived.

Who was playing what?

I don't know how many miles I traveled that day.

I crossed the city, up and down and across.

At the end, the night, I sat down on the grass, facing the pond.

The calm of nature has no equal.

We resource ourselves there, looking away at the grass at the centenary trees which will survive us and shelter families.

I stayed over there for hours. I wasn't hungry. Furthermore, I wasn't thirsty. I would rather not talk to any human. Only animals found favor in my eyes : birds, ducks, dogs, cats…

But I had to go back. Again. Those holidays were getting unforgettable, in the wrong sense of the word.

The following days were vapid. I went to bed earlier and earlier, empty, indifferent to everything.

Until that famous evening, Manuel called me, paralyzed as a child afraid of the dark : Thomas fell down the stairs and died.

I dropped the hand step. I didn't know what to think.

Was I happy? Was I relieved? Was I sad? I didn't know. I went to Manuel.

Paramedics had already taken the body. He was crying, as if I was going to take him in my arms to comfort him!

Two days later, I went to the car dealership to assess the extent of the damage, and I was surprised to discover Manuel in Thomas'office.

He was giving orders to all.

He was embarrassed to see me there, sputtered an apology, which I didn't listen to.

Likewise, he offered me his help for the cremation.

In contrast, I heard this last sentence.

I asked him again what he was doing here, he explained he was going to save the company, he will buy the company after I have managed the estate of the deceased. He knew a well-qualified friend, able to rebuild this business. The transaction will yield me a large sum, and all the administrative and financial issues caused by my husband will be away.

I had to think it over. And it's true that I had never had my thoughts so clear.

I took my car to the police station, where I explained they had to do an autopsy. I discussed the love connection of these two men, about the medication given by Manuel, a competent professional who was also his official lover for several weeks.

Not only that, but I proposed the police to ask about the company staff, the customers, to have an idea of his sudden change in behavior lately.

His fall couldn't be accidental. His lover already took his ease in the company, poking one of his "friends".

There was an autopsy. Weeks and months passed.

Manuel escaped justice.

Thomas took his secret to his grave, and I stayed in this world, neither alive nor dead.

I went back to work, the heart, and the spirit elsewhere.

One morning, on the way to work, I was passing near Manuel's house, as usual, when I saw two police officers handcuffing Manual.

He was going to pay for the death of Thomas.

But none will pay for my baby's death.

I came back to an empty house, I locked the door behind me.

I took a deliciously scented bath, soft music on a loop, and candles.

One week after, we could look in the local press that a Spanish teacher, who was greatly appreciated by her students, recently widowed and inconsolable, has committed suicide in her bathroom.

26

www.ingramcontent.com/pod-product-compliance
Lightning Source LLC
LaVergne TN
LVHW010904200726
843508LV00012B/2976